OTHER YEARLING BOOKS YOU WILL ENJOY:

WRITE UP A STORM WITH THE POLK STREET SCHOOL,
Patricia Reilly Giff
COUNT YOUR MONEY WITH THE POLK STREET SCHOOL,
Patricia Reilly Giff
THE POSTCARD PEST, *Patricia Reilly Giff*
TURKEY TROUBLE, *Patricia Reilly Giff*
SHOW TIME AT THE POLK STREET SCHOOL, *Patricia Reilly Giff*
THE BEAST IN MS. ROONEY'S ROOM, *Patricia Reilly Giff*
CODY AND QUINN, SITTING IN A TREE, *Kirby Larson*
SECOND-GRADE PIG PALS, *Kirby Larson*
PURELY ROSIE PEARL, *Patricia A. Cochrane*
THE PUPPY SISTER, *S. E. Hinton*

YEARLING BOOKS are designed especially to entertain and enlighten young people. Patricia Reilly Giff, consultant to this series, received her bachelor's degree from Marymount College and a master's degree in history from St. John's University. She holds a Professional Diploma in Reading and a Doctorate of Humane Letters from Hofstra University. She was a teacher and reading consultant for many years, and is the author of numerous books for young readers.

Annie Bananie
Moves to Barry Avenue

Leah Komaiko

illustrated by
Abby Carter

A Yearling Book

Published by
Bantam Doubleday Dell Books for Young Readers
a division of
Bantam Doubleday Dell Publishing Group, Inc.
1540 Broadway
New York, New York 10036

Visit us on the Web! www.bdd.com

Educators and librarians, visit the BDD Teacher's Resource Center at www.bdd.com/teachers

ISBN: 0-440-41035-5

Reprinted by arrangement with Delacorte Press

Printed in the United States of America

January 1998

10   9   8   7   6   5   4   3

CWO

For Jenny Tash

Chapter

1

"Give me quiet or give me death!" Libby Johnson yelled. She was sick of the noise. She was sick of her big brother, Carl, who was making the noise. She was sick of summer vacation. She was sick of everything.

Carl was practicing the piano. Now he was banging on the keys so hard, Libby could see the windows shaking.

"You're driving me crazy!" Libby yelled louder. She smiled. She liked the sound of her own loud voice, even if Carl couldn't hear her.

1

"Aggh," Grandma Gert said. She shook her finger at Libby. "What's the matter with you?"

Grandma Gert lived with the Johnsons. Grandma Gert was half deaf. Nobody knew from day to day what Grandma Gert could hear and what she couldn't. Today Grandma Gert couldn't hear the piano, but she did hear Libby yelling. Grandma Gert hated yelling.

"If you want to shout like a wild animal, why don't you go outside?"

"It's boring out there," Libby argued. "If I had a dog, at least I'd have somebody to play with."

"Dog shmog," Grandma Gert said. "Go play with all your friends. You've got a paradise outside on your very own block."

Grandma Gert didn't understand anything. Libby lived on Barry Avenue. But it should have been named Boring Avenue.

There were only three kids to play with on the street. Their names were Nina, Bonnie, and Debbie. But they were more like animals. All Nina cared about was being a horse. Bonnie pretended she was a cat, and Debbie grunted like a pig. Nice friends if you didn't mind living in a barnyard. Mostly they were boring. For now, though, nobody was in sight.

Then Libby's mother pulled into the driveway.

"Hello, Cookie Pie," Mrs. Johnson said. "Can you help me carry in groceries?"

"Okay," Libby said. "But then can I have a dog?"

Libby's mother gave her a look.

Libby watched her mother trying to lift the groceries. Mrs. Johnson was pregnant. It was so embarrassing. Lately she always looked tired and fat. In three weeks she was going to have the baby. The baby was a boy.

Libby didn't want another brother. She didn't even want a sister. What Libby really wanted was a dog.

Grandma Gert came out to help with the groceries.

"But, Mommy," Libby said, "after the baby is born can't I have a dog?"

"Not if I'm still breathing," Grandma Gert said. "If I ever see a dog in this house I'll flush it down the toilet."

Libby brought in a bag of groceries. Then she heard a loud noise.

Libby ran outside and looked across the street. A huge moving van was screeching to a halt. Somebody was moving into the house across the way. Two men started to unload the van.

Libby saw a girl with curly red hair. She looked like she was Libby's age. The girl marched down the moving van's ramp. And walking right behind the girl was the largest dog Libby had ever seen.

The girl talked to her dog. "Bark, Boris." Boris barked. His bark was huge. "Sit, Boris!" Boris sat. "Now watch me!" the girl commanded.

Then she ran up the moving van's ramp. When she got to the top, she did one perfect cartwheel after another all the way down to the bottom of the ramp.

Libby hid behind her house and watched everything. She couldn't believe it. Libby had never done one single perfect cartwheel. She wondered if this new girl was going to be in her grade. She hoped not. It would be too humiliating.

But then the girl saw Libby. Libby knew it was too late to look away. The girl stared at Libby. Libby stared back. The girl started running toward Libby. Boris ran right by her side.

Libby could see that the girl had big, bright eyes. Boris had the kind of teeth that looked like they could rip through flesh in one bite.

Libby's heart pounded. For a moment the girl, Boris, and Libby all just stood there. Then the girl smiled. She smiled the biggest smile anybody had ever smiled at Libby. Boris smiled, too. Life on boring Barry Avenue was about to change.

Chapter
2

"I'm Annie Bananie," the girl said. She had a big, friendly voice. "Do you want to play with me?"

"Okay," Libby said. She looked at Boris. She was trying not to act too excited.

"Oh, goody!" Annie said. She was very excited. "What's your name?"

"Libby Johnson," Libby said. "It doesn't rhyme or anything. I like your dog. Can I pet him?"

"Of course," Annie Bananie said. "He's superfriendly. Boris, this is our new friend, Libby. Give Libby paw."

Boris shook hands. Then he drooled on Libby's foot.

"Is this your house?" Annie asked. "Can we come in to play?"

Libby looked to make sure Grandma Gert wasn't looking out the window.

"It's just an ordinary house," Libby said. "Want to see something more fun?"

"Sure," Annie said. "Follow me!" Annie acted like she had lived on Barry Avenue for years.

"I'm going to Nichols School," Annie said.

"That's where I go," Libby said.

"I'm going to be in Mrs. Liebling's class," Annie said.

"She's my teacher, too," Libby said, smiling.

"Oh, wow!" Annie said. "I'm so lucky! Do you have a dog that Boris can play with?"

"No," Libby said. "But I'm probably going to get one."

"Oh, goody!" Annie laughed. "Then we'll have everything the same."

"Except you've got the best name," Libby said. "Is it real?"

"No," Annie said. "I made it up. My name was Ann. But that's so boring. Come on. Let's run!"

For the first time all day, Libby felt happy. She ran after Annie Bananie and Boris all the way to their new house.

"Mommy!" Annie Bananie called. "Quick, hurry! I have a new friend!"

Libby liked Annie's mother. Her name was Joy.

"I'm so happy to meet you," Joy said to Libby.

Then she shook Libby's hand like Libby was a businesswoman. Libby liked that.

"Come on in, Libby," Joy said. "Just step over the boxes."

Libby followed Annie Bananie. Annie had the best room. The phone man was putting in Annie's own phone line. The moving man brought in Annie's computer and two crates of tapes. Annie had about a thousand dresses and hats. She also had two rats named Walnut and Peanut, a hamster, and an old cat. And best of all, Libby thought, Annie had Boris and no brothers. No piano. No grandmother. Nobody making a lot of noise. Annie's father wasn't there. Libby figured he was at work.

"Let's go," Annie said to Libby. Boris's ears perked up.

"We're leaving," Annie sang out to her mother.

"Put on something clean and pretty," Joy called out from the living room. "And don't go too far."

"Oh, brother!" Annie rolled her eyes. Then she pulled a perfect white T-shirt out of her closet and changed as fast as she could.

"Follow me!" she said.

Libby couldn't figure out where Annie was going.

"Aye, Matey Boris," Annie called out. "Grab a fishing pole."

Boris picked up a stick off the ground and followed Annie. She was headed straight for the alley.

Libby never went into the alley except when she was throwing out the garbage. Now Libby couldn't believe it. There was Annie Bananie hanging halfway inside a garbage can.

"Aye, Matey Libby," Annie called. "Hand me Boris's pole, please."

At first Annie used the fishing pole to dig deeper and deeper into the garbage can. Then she called out, "Boris! Prepare the deck!"

Annie slowly lifted something up on the pole like she was reeling it in. At the end of the pole, Libby saw somebody's old necklace. It was filthy and made out of blue plastic that was supposed to look sparkly.

"Oh my gosh!" Annie said. Her face lit up. She spread the necklace out on the palms of her hands so that Libby and Boris could see.

"Look, Mateys!" Annie said. "Diamonds!"

She poured the necklace slowly into Libby's hands.

"Aye, Matey," Annie said. "This is for you. My first new friend. Treasure it always."

Chapter
3

Libby couldn't wait to tell everybody about Annie Bananie. But she couldn't show them the necklace Annie had given her. They would never understand. Libby wasn't sure she understood, herself. All she knew was that the necklace meant something important. Libby hid it under her pillow. Then she went downstairs for dinner.

Dinner was Libby's favorite time of day, even though her mother was not a very good cook. Libby liked it when her father came home from work and they all ate together.

Carl sat across from Libby. He put the fingers of one hand down on the table like he was playing the piano and held his fork with the other. When he thought nobody was looking, he flung a piece of potato off his fork right at Libby's face.

"Rodent," Libby said, giggling.

"Aggh," Grandma Gert said. She caught the potato in her hand and popped it into her mouth. Mr. Johnson didn't look up from his plate.

"So what's new, Cookie Pie?" he finally asked Libby.

"A girl moved in across the street," Libby said. "Her name is Annie Bananie."

"You ate what?" Grandma Gert asked.

"*Annie Bananie,*" Libby said loudly. She was being careful not to yell. But she didn't have to worry. Grandma Gert couldn't hear a thing.

Libby told the family about Annie Bananie.

"And she has the greatest dog," Libby said. "He's a rottweiler. I don't have to have one that big, but can't I at least have a small dog?"

"Dog?" Suddenly Grandma Gert could hear again. "Did somebody say *dog*? If I ever see a dog in this house, I'll flush it down the toilet!"

The next morning Libby got her necklace out of its hiding place. She slipped it carefully into her pocket. Then she went over to Annie Bananie's house. Right before she got to Annie's door, she slipped the necklace over her head. It looked dirtier than yesterday, but Libby was proud to wear it.

"Oh, goody!" Annie said when she saw Libby at the door. "Boris, look who's here." Boris barked.

"I'm so lucky you're my friend," Annie said. "What should we do today?"

"What do you want to do?" Libby asked.

"Let's break out of this jailhouse," Annie said, laughing. "Let's start a club!"

"You, me, and Boris?" Libby asked.

"And we need some other kids, too," Annie said.

"Yeah, great," Libby said. "But I'm warning you. There's nobody good on Barry Avenue to start a club with."

But Annie didn't hear Libby. She and Boris were already running ahead when Nina Blaskewitz came galloping out of her garage. Her thin, greasy hair was flopping back and forth on her face like an old horse's mane.

More than anything, Nina wanted to be a horse. She wanted a horse, but all her parents got her was a collie they named Mr. Ed. Nina had about a thousand plastic horses that hung over her bed. But she never let Mr. Ed in her room.

Grandma Gert always said Nina's parents needed to take Nina to have her head examined. Libby didn't mind Nina, but she never once cared about being a horse.

"Whoa! Hi, Libby!" Nina called out. She galloped faster. Libby pretended she didn't see Nina. She hoped Annie hadn't seen Nina either, but she had.

"Hi-giddyup!" Nina called out. She slapped herself on the leg and ran to catch up with Libby and Annie.

"Who's that?" Annie asked.

"Nina," Libby answered.

"What's the matter with her?" Annie asked. Libby had never seen Annie so quiet.

"Neigh," Nina said before Libby could answer. Then Nina shook her head from side to side. She made sounds with her nose like a horse that was tired and needed water. Boris barked and pulled hard on his leash.

"Heel, Boris," Annie said. That was all she could say— "Heel."

"Whoa!" Nina said. "Are you the new girl?"

"Yes," Annie answered. She couldn't take her eyes off Nina.

Nina trotted around in a circle. She kicked up mud with her shoes like they were hooves. Annie just stood there. Libby didn't know what to do. She felt so embarrassed by Nina.

Nina shook her head one final time. Then she started trotting slowly back toward her house. Annie turned to Libby.

"I'm so lucky you're my friend, Libby," she said.

"I tried to warn you," Libby said with a smile. Now she and Annie and Boris could have their own club after all.

But then Nina stopped trotting. She started to gallop. And before Libby could look up, Annie was galloping right behind her.

"Hi-yaa!" Annie called out at the top of her lungs.

"Hi-yaa! Do it like this! On your side!" Nina called. "It works better."

Annie galloped on one side. "You're right, this is the more fun way," she called. Then she shook her head back and forth.

"Neigh! I'm Annie Bananie!"

"Neigh! I'm Nina."

"Want to be in our club?" Annie asked.

"Neigh!" Nina answered. She shook her head up and down.

"Come on, Boris," Nina called. "Annie Bananie, do you like horses?"

"Neigh," Annie said. And she looked behind her to make sure Libby was still there.

"Giddyup, Libby," Annie called.

"Hi-giddyup," Libby called back. And then, for the first time in Libby Johnson's life, she galloped down Barry Avenue.

Chapter
4

They would have galloped all day if it hadn't been for Bonnie. Through her window, Bonnie saw Nina, Annie, and Libby coming, and she ran outside. She hid behind the bushes.

"Hi-giddyup!" Nina called.

"Giddyup hi!" Annie followed behind her.

Boris's paw crossed the first crack in Bonnie's sidewalk, and then, suddenly, *"Meeooww!"*

Bonnie sprang out from behind the bushes. *"Meowwwwww!"* she screamed.

Boris jumped back and whined. Nina pulled in on her reins fast.

"Hissssssss." Bonnie shot her arm out at Nina like it had a claw at the end of it. "Hissssss." Bonnie laughed. Then she scrunched up her face so that she looked completely ugly, even though she was the prettiest girl in their class.

Libby stopped. She wasn't really afraid of Bonnie, but she never really wanted to play with her, either. Especially now. Bonnie always had to have everything her own way. Now Libby was just ashamed. Ashamed of Barry Avenue.

"Meowww." Bonnie purred at Annie Bananie.

"Neigh," Nina wheezed. She trotted in a circle around the rosebush.

"Ruff," Boris barked. His bark was huge.

"Heel," Annie said. She pulled hard on Boris's leash. That was all she could say— "Heel."

Bonnie didn't take her eyes off Annie Bananie. Libby felt nervous. Maybe Bonnie was going to attack Annie Bananie. Or worse—maybe Annie was about to run off with Bonnie and turn into a cat.

Libby had to do something fast. Suddenly she looked up and saw Debbie. Debbie was the last of the three friends on Barry Avenue. She was riding her bike. She pedaled and at the same time pushed her glasses up on her nose. She had a book in her basket.

"Oink, you guys," she called. "What are you doing?"

"Meeoooowwwwww." Bonnie forced a yawn when she saw Debbie. "Boring . . ." Of the three girls, Debbie was Libby's favorite. Debbie didn't care that much about being an animal. Sometimes she grunted like a pig, but mostly she just liked reading books.

"We were playing horse," Nina said.

"I'm Debbie," Debbie said to Annie. She pushed her glasses up on her nose.

"Hello, Debbie." Annie Bananie smiled.

Libby felt good again, like everything was going to be okay. She didn't have to worry. Bonnie wasn't acting too much like an alley cat today. Annie Bananie and Bonnie were never going to be best friends. Any second, Nina would go trotting home, and Debbie was just Debbie.

"Meow." Bonnie stretched and arched her back like a cat. Then she smiled so that Annie could see how white her teeth were. "Meoowwww."

"Neigh," Nina wheezed.

"Annie Bananie and I are starting a club," Libby announced proudly. She played with her necklace. She decided that now was her chance to take charge.

"And Boris, too," Annie reminded her.

"Is that your dog?" Debbie asked Annie.

"No, it's her cat," Bonnie said with a sneer. Then she scratched Boris under his chin like she wasn't even afraid he could bite her hand off. Boris liked it.

"Boris, Annie, and I are starting a club," Libby said again quickly.

"What kind of a club?" Bonnie asked.

"The fun kind, of course, Bonnie," Annie said, laughing. Her laugh was big and friendly.

"A cat club!" Bonnie jumped in.

"Horses!" Nina said, talking into the front of her shirt.

"You got a problem, Nina?" Bonnie asked. "Nobody has a horse!" Then Bonnie smiled at Annie Bananie.

"Let's do something different!" Libby said. "We always do the same club!"

"We've never had a club before," Debbie said. Then she opened her book. Debbie was right. Libby had to think fast on her feet. She looked down. Boris was drooling on her shoe.

"Dogs!" she shouted. "Let's start a dog club!"

"That's perfect, Libby!" Annie Bananie said. "Bark, Boris!"

Boris barked.

"Neigh." Nina smiled at Annie. "I have a dog. His name is Mr. Ed."

"See, Boris?" Annie hugged Boris close to her. "I told you you would love everybody at the new house! We're so lucky to have all these new friends!"

"And I know the perfect thing we can call ourselves," Libby said quickly.

"The Barry Avenue Bowwows," Nina said.

"Boring Avenue," Bonnie said. She licked her arm like a cat cleaning itself. "And don't call me a bowwow. I'm a beauty!" Bonnie laughed and poufed up her hair like she was posing for a magazine. Annie Bananie laughed, too.

"That's it!" Libby said quickly. "We'll call ourselves the Boris Avenue Beauties."

"Perfect!" Annie shouted. "You're so smart, Libby."

"I know." Libby giggled.

"Hey, wait a second," Bonnie hissed. She looked Libby right in the eye. "You're the only one of us who doesn't have a dog! How can you be in a dog club if you don't even have a dog?"

Nobody had thought of that. Annie had Boris. Nina had Mr. Ed. Bonnie had a boxer named Cleo. Cleo was blind in both eyes, but she still counted. And Debbie had Max, even though Max looked more like a mean little rat on a leash.

"I might get a dog right after my baby brother is born," Libby heard herself say.

"What kind?" Bonnie laughed. "A hot dog?"

"No, a real dog, Cats-up Girl," Libby said.

"Your grandmother hates dogs," Nina added.

"No she doesn't," Libby protested.

"I say Libby should still be in our club even if she doesn't have her dog yet," Annie said. "After all, she was the one who thought of the dog club idea."

Libby smiled. "I hereby declare that the Boris Avenue Beauties will now have their first official meeting," she said.

"Who made you president, Libby?" Bonnie wanted to know.

"Boris should be president," Nina neighed to Annie. "He's the biggest dog."

"You should be president." Debbie smiled at Annie Bananie. "You have the best name!"

"If it wasn't for Annie Bananie we wouldn't be having a club at all," Libby said. Then Annie and Libby smiled at each other.

"I want Libby to be president," Annie said. Her voice was big and happy.

"Whatever Annie wants," Libby said. "Because she's the new girl."

"Whatever the new girl wants," Bonnie said, imitating Libby. "But if Libby gets to be our president I want her to have to do something to prove herself worthy, Annie Bananie."

Annie Bananie's face lit up. "That's a great idea!" she said. "It will be like an initiation. When we each have our turn to be president, we have to do something special."

Libby's heart pounded. What would she have to do?

Everybody stood there trying to think of an idea.

"I've got it!" Debbie said slowly. "To be president of the Boris Avenue Beauties, Libby has to get her grandma to kiss Boris."

"Where?" Libby said, panicking. "At my house?"

"Mmm-hmmm." Debbie nodded. She

pushed her glasses up on her nose. "And it has to be on the mouth."

"For once you're a genius, Debbie!" Bonnie meowed. Then Libby looked at Debbie, and Debbie looked at Libby.

"Oink." Debbie grunted like a pig. That was all she could say—"Oink."

Chapter

5

"Food's on, Your Majesty!" Libby yelled into the living room. Carl was playing the piano.

"I said it's time for dinner, Carl," Libby yelled even louder. "What are you, deaf?"

The telephone rang. Libby answered it. "It's for you, Grandma!" she yelled.

Libby helped her mother bring the food to the table.

"Annie and I started a club today," Libby said. "And I'm the president."

"Libby for president." Mrs. Johnson smiled. Today her stomach was so big she could hardly fit in her chair.

"Wow, Cookie Pie," Mr. Johnson said. "I guess boring Barry Avenue isn't so boring."

"Yeah." Libby giggled. "The first meeting is tomorrow at Bonnie's house, but then our meeting has to be here the next day in the afternoon. Okay?"

"The next day after tomorrow is Friday," Mrs. Johnson said. "Did you forget? Friday morning Daddy and I are going away for the weekend. It's our last chance to have a little vacation before the baby comes."

"Oh," Libby said. "I forgot."

"But if Grandma Gert gets back from her card game in time, I don't see why you can't have the meeting here," Mrs. Johnson said. "Just as long as you don't do anything that will upset her. You know what I'm talking about."

"We'll behave," Libby said.

Grandma Gert hung up the phone. Everybody could tell she was in a bad mood. Libby didn't care. Libby had problems of her own. And Grandma Gert was at the top of the list.

"Aggh," Grandma Gert said without looking up from her plate. "I could use some potatoes."

"Is something wrong?" Mrs. Johnson asked. She handed Grandma Gert the bowl.

Grandma Gert waved her arms like she was shooing away flies. Then she put a forkful of potatoes in her mouth.

"I don't want to talk about it," Grandma Gert said. "Thirty years we play cards on Fridays at Sally's. Now she just called to say they've all decided this week we play on Saturday. Before you know, it will be Sunday. Then Tuesday."

"What's wrong with some change?" Libby's father wanted to know.

"Plenty!" Grandma Gert reached for more potatoes. "I was the one who started this club. I'm the president. I don't have to prove anything to them. If they don't want me to play anymore, why don't they just tell me?"

"Does that mean you'll be home on Friday?" Libby asked.

"Of course!" Grandma Gert said. "And I may not go on Saturday, either."

"Don't be silly," Mrs. Johnson said. "These are your friends. They love you."

"Yeah, Grandma," Carl said. "Why don't you just kiss and make up?"

"Aagh." Grandma Gert laughed. "I'd rather kiss a dog."

Libby looked up from her plate. Then she smiled.

That night Libby couldn't fall asleep. She couldn't think how she'd ever get Grandma Gert to kiss Boris. She decided she would go to Annie Bananie's early the next day.

They could make a plan together before they had to go to the meeting at Bonnie's. At last Libby fell asleep.

But when she rang Annie's doorbell the next morning, Libby didn't hear Boris. She couldn't hear anybody inside Annie's house. Finally Joy came to the door.

"Good morning, honey." Annie's mother smiled. She shook Libby's hand. "Annie and Boris just left with Bonnie. She came over to pick them up early for your meeting."

Then Joy looked down at Libby's necklace. "Pretty," Joy said, smiling.

"Thank you," Libby said.

Libby started over to Bonnie's. Annie Bananie had already forgotten about her. Libby looked down at her stupid necklace. How dumb could she be? What good did it do to be picked as president if all that meant was you got to wear a piece of garbage around your neck?

Chapter

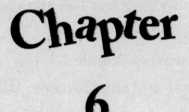

6

"Hi!" Annie said the second she saw Libby. Annie gave Libby one of her biggest smiles. Libby tried not to feel happy inside. She just looked at Annie. Today Annie was wearing perfect white overalls. Boris had on a new white collar.

"Meowww." Bonnie came into the room. She smiled at Libby like Bonnie hadn't done a single thing wrong.

"Last night at dinner my grandma said she'd kiss a dog," Libby said.

"That's good," Bonnie said. "Because Annie and I decided if you can't get your grandma to kiss Boris I'm the next candidate for president."

"Don't worry, Bonnie," Libby said. She looked right at Annie Bananie. "I'll still be president."

"Meowww, well, today I'm president of the Welcoming Committee," Bonnie said. "I made a special welcome cake for the new girl. Annie was helping me. But first . . ."

Bonnie started setting the table with a pretty lady's tea set at each place. That's how Bonnie liked everything. Pretty. Bonnie had on a pink party dress and patent-leather sandals. Her hair was pinned up on the top of her head in a perfect braid.

Libby could hardly wait for Debbie and Nina to show up. They would be normal.

"Neigh," Nina said when she got to the door. She threw her head from side to side so that everybody could see she had washed her hair for the first time in a month. Then she trotted into the living room. Debbie was right behind her. Debbie was just Debbie.

"The Boris Avenue Beauties meeting will now begin!" Libby raised her arm.

"So what are we going to do today, Ms. President?" Annie asked.

"Who says she gets to pick what we do?" Bonnie asked. "It's my house. I should decide."

"But the president always decides," Annie Bananie said.

"Meowww," Bonnie mumbled. "Whatever the new girl wants."

"Let the president bring the meeting to order," Annie said.

Suddenly Libby realized she hadn't thought of a single thing they could do. She had been too busy worrying about Grandma Gert.

"We're a dog club," Libby finally said. "We should do something special today for our dogs."

Boris barked. He was the only dog there except for Bonnie's blind dog, Cleo. Boris tried to play with Cleo, but all Cleo could do was bark and run into the wall. Bonnie couldn't stop laughing.

"Meowww, let's just come to the table for refreshments," Bonnie said. She was trying to sound like a grown-up lady. She poured milk into each dainty little teacup. Everybody followed Bonnie over to the table. Libby didn't even feel like a president anymore.

"Time for the special cake," Bonnie said. She jumped up and started for the kitchen. "Meow, nobody's allowed to come in here but me. I'm going to put on a surprise topping."

Suddenly Libby had a feeling in her stomach that Bonnie was up to no good.

Bonnie came out of the kitchen carrying the cake. Boris went to her side. Libby just kept her eye on Bonnie.

Bonnie put a piece of cake on everyone's plate. Bonnie gave Annie the best piece—the only one with sparkles on top. Libby's mouth started to water. She couldn't wait to eat her piece of cake. Boris came and sat next to Libby. He stared right at Libby's cake and panted. Libby took a bite of cake. It was delicious. Maybe Bonnie wasn't up to anything after all.

"Everyone eat," Libby said. She smiled at Bonnie. Bonnie looked pleased.

"No thank you," Annie said. "I don't want any cake."

"Why not?" Bonnie seemed upset. "But you have to!"

"I'm not hungry now," Annie said.

Debbie and Nina looked up from their plates. They had frosting all over their faces.

"You should have told me before," Bonnie said. "I gave you the best piece."

"She's right, Annie Bananie," Nina said, looking over at Annie's plate. "It's got special sparkle topping."

"I'll eat it," Debbie offered.

"Don't be such a pig," Nina said to her.

"I get to have Annie's piece," Libby said. "I'm the president."

"Why don't you all share my piece?" Annie asked.

"No way. It's supposed to be for you," Bonnie meowed at Annie.

"I don't want it," Annie Bananie meowed back.

And while they were doing that, Nina grabbed Annie's cake. She took a bite.

"Mmmm," she said.

"Give a bite to Boris," Libby insisted.

"Meowwww." Bonnie giggled. "Give a bite to Boris." And she reached over to Nina's plate.

"No!" Annie shouted at Bonnie. But it was too late.

"Help!" Nina suddenly spit a chocolatey wad of cake out of her mouth. She pushed the plate off the table. She threw her head from side to side.

"I've been poisoned!" Nina screamed. *"I've been poisoned!"*

"You're going to die!" Debbie cried. "Poison is fatal if swallowed!"

"Don't eat any of that cake, Boris!" Annie shouted.

Boris barked. Cleo barked. Then she ran into the wall.

"Meooww!" Bonnie laughed. Libby had never seen Bonnie have such a good time. "It's only kitty litter," she squealed. "The sparkly topping is just colored kitty litter."

"I swallowed kitty litter!" Nina wheezed.

"I could have eaten kitty litter!" Debbie cried. "Was it used?"

"Don't be disgusting," Bonnie said. "It was

a fresh batch. It's a new sparkly kitty litter. Isn't it pretty? I only put a little bit on that one piece. Don't worry, you won't die, Nina."

Then Annie Bananie looked at Bonnie. And Bonnie looked at Annie. They both knew who that cake was supposed to be for.

The next thing anyone knew, Bonnie had pulled Annie Bananie down to the floor.

"Hisssss." Bonnie shot her arm out at Annie.

"Hisssss." Annie shot her arm back.

"Meooowww!" Bonnie grabbed at Annie's shoe. She dug her fingernails into Annie's ankle.

"Ouch!" Annie Bananie fell to the carpet. Then she reached over and yanked Bonnie's clip out of her hair.

"Meooowwww!" Bonnie screamed. She grabbed Annie's arm and bit it.

"Yeowwww!" Annie cried.

"*Ruff!*" Boris barked at Bonnie. His bark was huge.

"Stop it, Bonnie!" Debbie squealed. "Why do you have to ruin everything?"

"She started it," Bonnie hissed at Debbie.

"And I'll finish it!" Annie said.

She forced Bonnie down on her stomach. Then Annie sat on Bonnie and pinned Bonnie's arm behind her.

"Oink." Debbie giggled.

"Stop!" Bonnie yelled at Annie. "You're killing me."

Bonnie struggled with all her might until she knocked Annie off her. Then Bonnie jumped up and sat on Annie.

"You give?" Bonnie asked, pinning Annie's arm behind her.

"Peace!" Libby yelled out. She liked the sound of her own loud voice, even though nobody listened.

"I said peace!" she shouted again. "I'm the president. You have to do what I say!"

Boris climbed on top of Bonnie and Annie Bananie. He put his big paws on Bonnie's back. Then he started licking.

"No, Boris." Annie started to giggle. "Go on. Get off!"

"He's licking me to death." Bonnie laughed and rolled off Annie.

Annie Bananie sat on the floor laughing.

"The meeting is officially over," Libby announced.

"When's the next meeting?" Nina cheered like she had already forgotten she'd almost died ten minutes ago.

"Tomorrow at Libby's. And it will be even more fun," Annie said. Her voice was big and happy.

"Don't forget to bring Boris, Annie," Debbie said, and oinked.

"Meow, Libby." Bonnie laughed. "Don't

forget to bring your grandma."

"I'm sorry," Bonnie said to Annie. "I was just playing. Truce?"

"Truce," Annie Bananie said. "Besides, that was almost sort of fun!"

"I know," Bonnie said. "We can always have fun at my house."

Everybody got up to leave.

"You'd better get lucky tomorrow, Libby," Bonnie said. "You'd just better get lucky!"

Chapter 7

Annie, Boris, and Libby walked home alone together.

"Want me to come over early tomorrow?" Annie asked. "That way your grandma can get to know Boris before it's time to kiss him."

"No, that's okay," Libby said. She looked down at the sidewalk. She didn't know what to do. She wished Grandma Gert would die before tomorrow. Then she wished she hadn't wished that.

"What's wrong?" Annie Bananie asked.

"I don't think my grandma wants to kiss Boris," Libby said. She spoke fast because she was afraid she would start to cry.

"When she sees how friendly he is, she will," Annie said. "I promise. Besides, it will be good practice for when you get your own dog. Believe me, he'll want to kiss your grandmother all the time."

"Well, that's what I forgot to tell you," Libby said.

"What?" Annie asked. She looked at Libby.

"I'm sorry." Libby burst into tears. "I don't think I'm getting my own dog. Do you hate me for life?"

"Of course I don't." Annie Bananie hugged Libby.

Boris smiled. Then he drooled on Libby's foot.

"So is it true your grandma really is a dog-hater?" Annie asked.

"Yes!" Libby cried.

"That's okay," Annie said. "You can still be our president. We just have to tell Grandma Gert the truth."

"Are you kidding?" Libby asked. "You don't know my grandmother. She's the meanest person on earth. She won't even pet a dog."

"But once she sees Boris, I promise she'll love him," Annie said.

"It's hopeless," Libby said. "Bonnie can be president."

"Are you sure your grandma wouldn't kiss Boris even if she knew you'd be president of our club?"

"She wouldn't kiss Boris even if she thought I'd be president of the United States," Libby said.

"Oh well," Annie said. "Then if we can't tell her the truth there's only one thing left to do."

"What's that?" Libby asked.

"Be at my house tomorrow morning early before the meeting," Annie said.

"Why?" Libby asked.

"Your grandma will want to kiss Boris," Annie said. "Believe me. Boris and I will think of a plan."

"Okay, but you're not going to let Bonnie come to your house early too, are you?" Libby asked.

"No, Madam President," Annie said, laughing. "Trust me."

Chapter

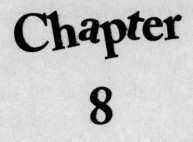

8

Friday morning when Libby woke up, the house was quiet. She ran to the kitchen to see what time it was. There was a note on the table:

Good morning, Cookie Pie.

Daddy and I didn't want to wake you before we left. Have fun today! I know I can count on you to lead a good meeting that won't disturb Grandma Gert. We'll be home tomorrow night.

Love,

Mom

Libby got dressed fast and started across the street to Annie Bananie's house.

"You're up early, honey," Joy said when she came to the door. "Is something wrong?"

"Annie and I have to prepare early for our meeting," Libby said. "Didn't she tell you?"

"No." Joy tried not to smile. "In fact, I haven't heard a sound out of Annie's room yet. You can take a peek if you want."

"Thank you," Libby said. She played with her necklace.

Libby wondered why she would risk getting killed to be president when all being president meant was that you had to wake everybody else up.

"Shhh!" Annie jumped out of bed.

"Ruf—" Boris started to bark.

"No, shhh, Boris, no bark!" Annie commanded.

Boris looked at Libby. He lay down.

56

"That's my good boy." Annie patted Boris. "Here's a cookie."

Libby giggled. "Why are you whispering?"

"I'm teaching Boris to be quiet," Annie said.

"That's good," Libby said. "But we've got to get ready for the meeting."

"What do you think we're doing?" Annie asked. "I'm training him for your grandma."

"She's already deaf," Libby said. "But she can still see!"

"Okay, but watch this! That was just one of his tricks!"

Annie pushed up her pajama sleeves. She stood up on her bed and tossed her slippers across the room.

"Slippers, please," Annie commanded. Boris looked at Libby. Then he fetched the slippers.

"That's my helpful boy." Annie kissed Boris. "See, Libby?" Annie asked. "He does a trick and I just naturally want to kiss him.

Your grandma will too. I've been teaching Boris helpful tricks all night. Watch this one!"

"That's okay," Libby said. "It's not that Boris isn't the smartest, but my grandma is stupid. She wouldn't care if Boris could fold the laundry. Trust me. It won't work. She'll never kiss him because he's a dog."

Libby tried to hide her disappointment.

"Oh well," Annie said. "Boris, I'm sorry." She scratched Boris's chin. "But I'm afraid you just can't be a dog!"

Libby thought Annie Bananie was losing it from being awake all night.

Then Annie ran to her closet.

"Help me, Matey," she called.

Annie pulled down two big boxes of hats, ribbons, a baggy shirt, and a handful of dresses. She threw them on her bed.

"There are plenty of hidden treasures in that closet, Matey," Annie said. "Trust me. Let's put this shirt on Boris!"

"Oh my gosh!" Libby laughed. "You're so lucky to have Boris!"

"*You're* so lucky," Annie Bananie said. "I wanted a baby brother, but my mom and dad got me Boris instead. Now he's my baby sister!"

Annie put a straw hat on Boris. "Borissa! Come here, Borissa—give me a kiss-a!"

Libby laughed so hard, she forgot to even care about being president. Annie Bananie knew the truth about Libby, and she still wanted to play. Libby didn't have to prove anything to Nina or Debbie. Bonnie could be the stupid president. Libby and Annie Bananie would still be friends. Libby felt good inside.

"Meowww, Annie Bananie." Bonnie smiled. "I came to invite Boris to play at my house with Cleo before the meeting. Dogs and their owners only."

"Thanks, but I'm afraid Boris isn't a dog anymore, Bonnie." Annie Bananie giggled.

"Oh, really?" Bonnie asked. "What's he supposed to be now, a cat?"

"He's a beauty!" Annie said. "Come on. Help me put on Borissa's booties. Or do you want to pick out some special jewelry? We want him to look real pretty."

"Meowww." Bonnie giggled. "Why don't you let Boris borrow your exquisite necklace, Libby? Where'd you get that thing from, anyway?" Bonnie laughed. "The garbage can?"

Libby and Annie Bananie looked at each other. Then they fell on the bed laughing. Bonnie just stood there.

"Meow, I don't see what's so funny. You guys are cheating."

"Who says we're cheating?" Libby laughed.

"Don't be mad, Bonnie," Annie Bananie said. "We're just playing."

"Maybe you called it playing where you used to live, but here on Planet Earth it's cheating. I should be automatic president because Libby's a cheater."

"I am not a cheater," Libby said.

"If it's not cheating for you to disguise Boris, then it's not cheating for me to go to your house right now and warn your grand-mother," Bonnie said, and meowed. "Okay?"

"My grandma's not even up yet!" Libby said.

"Meoowww." Bonnie smiled at Libby and Annie like a cat that had just swallowed a rat.

"Meoow." Annie Bananie smiled. "Go ahead!"

Chapter

9

"Why'd you say that?" Libby asked Annie Bananie. "You don't know Bonnie. Believe me. She'll do it!"

"Relax, Madam President," Annie Bananie said. "Trust me. Bonnie's not going to tell."

"Oh, I get it!" Libby patted Boris. "We let Bonnie tell my grandmother anything she wants. Then you come to my house without Boris and it makes Bonnie look like the liar she is. That's even better than being president! You're a genius! Bonnie's going to have a cow!"

"That's not why I said that—" Annie said.

Libby started for the door. "So hurry up and come over, Annie. Okay?"

"Okay," Annie said. Then Annie and Boris went back to the closet.

When Libby got home, Grandma Gert was in the kitchen.

"Where were you?" Grandma Gert asked.

"At Annie Bananie's," Libby answered.

"Sure, you can have a banana," Grandma Gert said. "I made potatoes. Come on. Eat your breakfast!"

"Bonnie didn't come over, did she?" Libby spoke louder.

"Which one is Bonnie?" Grandma Gert asked. "The horse who needs to have her head examined?"

"No, Grandma," Libby said. "The cat."

"Aggh," Grandma Gert said. "I don't know which one is crazier."

The doorbell rang. Nina trotted into the kitchen.

"Hello, Mrs. Johnson," Nina called loudly. "It's me, Nina Blaskewitz! I ate kitty litter yesterday. I'll eat dog food today if I have to."

Grandma Gert looked at Nina. Then she ate her potatoes.

"Can she hear me?" Nina asked.

"Who knows?" Libby said.

"Who knows who?" Grandma Gert asked.

"Oink." Debbie came to the door. "Did she kiss him yet?"

"Neigh." Nina galloped around the sofa.

Libby ran back to the kitchen. "Grandma, I didn't tell you something about today. And Bonnie's going to—"

"Just eat, Libby," Grandma Gert said. "Don't worry. For twenty years I've had my card club. Tomorrow for the first time in history we play on Saturday. Believe you me. There's nothing I haven't seen."

"Meowwwww." Bonnie scratched on the door. "Come on, everybody," she purred.

"I have a special surprise for Libby's grandma!"

"Is it that cake?" Nina asked.

"Wait!" Debbie pushed her glasses up on her nose. "We should wait for Annie Bananie and Bo——"

"No, it's okay," Libby said. She looked Bonnie right in the eye. "Trust me. Annie Bananie won't be mad."

"Hello, Libby's grandma," Bonnie said loudly. *"I suppose Libby didn't tell you what you're supposed to do today."*

"Don't tell her, Bonnie!" Nina neighed. "You'll ruin it."

"Go ahead," said Libby. She could tell right now Grandma Gert couldn't hear a thing.

"Libby said her grandma would kiss a dog, but they cheated. So she's about to kiss a girl named Boris!"

The doorbell rang. Everybody ran to the door.

"Aggh, Libby," Grandma Gert called. "It's too much noise. And which one is Boris, anyway?"

Chapter 10

"Oh my gosh, Boris!" Debbie screamed.

"Is he going to die?" Nina cried.

Libby's heart stopped. Boris's stomach was covered with bandages. There was a neck brace over his collar and a sheet around his head with blood on it.

"He was in an accident," Annie Bananie said sadly.

"Wasn't he wearing a seat belt?" Nina asked.

"Meow, what are you guys, dumb and dumber?" Bonnie asked. "That's not real blood!"

"It sure is," Libby said. "Boris better stay outside, Annie. My grandma doesn't allow blood on the carpet."

"Your grandma will feel sorry for Boris," Annie Bananie whispered. "Heel, gently, Boris."

Boris hobbled into the room. His front paw was in a wooden sling.

"He's faking!" Bonnie shouted.

Grandma Gert came into the room carrying a deck of cards. Everybody froze.

"Don't mind me," Grandma Gert said. "I'm going to play solitaire. I need to get another deck. I'm missing cards from this one."

Grandma Gert opened the cabinet. Then she looked up and . . .

"*Agghhh!*" Grandma Gert threw all the cards in the air.

Boris jumped. Then he hobbled after Grandma Gert.

"Get that dog out of here!" Grandma Gert screamed. *"I'm telling you. I'm going to have a heart attack!"*

"It's okay, Grandma." Libby ran after her. "I'm sorry. Don't be afraid!"

"Boris, heel!" Annie commanded.

Boris hobbled faster.

Grandma Gert ran to the broom closet. She tossed everything out of the closet. Everything but the broom.

"Where is that thing?" she shouted. "Aggh, never mind. I'll use this!"

Grandma Gert came out swinging the toilet plunger over her head.

"Please. Don't hurt Boris!" Annie called. "He just wants to kiss you!"

"Get out!" Grandma Gert swung the plunger at Boris.

"Meoww, everybody!" Bonnie screamed. "Run for your lives!"

Boris pulled off his splint and ran out the

door. Everyone ran out behind him. Annie Bananie just stood there looking at Grandma Gert. Grandma Gert looked at Annie Bananie.

"Did I just hear you say that dog wants to kiss me?" Grandma Gert said, catching her breath.

"Uh-huh." Annie Bananie smiled. "Would you like to? Boris is very gentle."

"Boris is gentle?" Grandma Gert raised her eyebrow. "Didn't my granddaughter tell you *I'm* not gentle? I don't even allow those dog things in my house. Believe you me. The last thing in this world I'll ever kiss is a dog!"

"Libby told me," Annie Bananie said. "Don't be mad. It's my fault. I tried every plan I could think of to make you want to kiss Boris. Because if you don't, Libby can't be president of our club. That's the rule! I promise Boris is clean. You just have to kiss him once. Can't you just change your mind?"

"Aggh, sweetheart." Grandma Gert wiped her forehead. "You can't teach an old dog new tricks."

Annie Bananie ran outside.

"Meowww!" Bonnie shouted. "Tomorrow we have to officially swear me in as the official president of the Boris Avenue Beauties! So whose house?"

Everybody looked at each other.

"Meow, you guys. Come on!"

"We can have the meeting here," Libby said. Her heart was pounding.

"It's okay, Libby," Annie Bananie said. "Trust me. Your grandma's not going to change her mind by tomorrow."

"Trust *me*." Libby smiled. "My grandma's not even going to be home tomorrow. She has her card club. In fact, nobody's going to be at my house tomorrow."

"Oh my gosh!" Debbie squealed.

"Meow, Libby," Bonnie said. "You're a good loser. Come on, everybody. Ready?"

"Two, four, six, eight!
Who do we appreciate?
Libby! Libby! Libby!"

Grandma Gert peeked out from behind the curtain.

"Aggh, Libby," Grandma Gert mumbled. "Kiss a dog."

Then she smiled.

Chapter

11

Saturday morning Libby and Grandma Gert sat at the breakfast table. Grandma Gert chewed on her cornflakes.

"Aggh," she said. "They call this stuff breakfast? I'm making a fresh pot of mashed potatoes. That's what I call delicious. How's your toast?"

Libby didn't say a word. She looked up at the clock. It was almost time for Grandma Gert to leave for her card game.

"I like your friend the Bananie girl," Grandma Gert said. "But I still can't believe you said I'd kiss a—"

"None of this would have happened if I could have just had a dog like everybody else!" Libby yelled. "But no! I'm not allowed to be normal. I'm not president of my club today. Are you happy?"

"No, not really," Grandma Gert said softly. "But if it makes you feel any better, I'm not going to be president of my club today, either. In fact, I'm not even going to go."

"What?" Libby's voice got quiet. "Why not?"

"It's Saturday. I've got better things to do!" Grandma Gert said. She got up from the table. She emptied the new pot of potatoes into a big wooden bowl. Then she put the bowl on the counter.

"But you've got to go," Libby said. "I'm sorry I yelled. But your friends are counting on you!"

"Aggh, you're right," Grandma Gert said. "I'll go call them and say I'm not coming."

"I have to use the phone first." Libby got up. "I forgot to tell Annie Bananie something."

"Sit," Grandma Gert said. "Finish your breakfast. Try some potatoes. They turned out beautiful."

Libby looked at the bowl. Her heart was beating fast. She listened to Grandma Gert laughing on the phone. Then Libby heard something terrifying. It was the sound of Boris's dog chains. Libby ran to the screen door, but it was too late.

"Good morning, Matey Libby. Coast is clear, right?" Annie skipped inside.

Grandma Gert walked into the kitchen.

"I'm off the phone," Grandma Gert called. And then she saw Boris.

"*Aagggghhh!*" she yelled. "*It's back! I can't believe that dog is in my house again!*"

Grandma Gert ran to the broom closet.

"Boris!" Libby yelled.

"Don't run, Grandma Gert!" Annie called. "Boris just thinks you want to play."

"Aggh!" Grandma Gert came out of the closet swinging the toilet plunger. "Does it look like I want to play?"

Then Grandma Gert ran after Boris. Boris turned and ran into the kitchen. He slid across the floor and up to the counter. Boris sniffed. He smelled something good. He jumped up on the counter. Then he shoved his face deep in Grandma Gert's mashed potatoes.

"Boris!" Annie hollered.

But before anyone could stop him, Boris had pulled the bowl down off the counter.

"*No!*" Grandma Gert cried.

Boris sat in a mound of mashed potatoes. Then he ran into the living room and hid under the piano.

Grandma Gert sat down in her chair slowly. "Will somebody please tell me I'm not losing my mind?" she said.

"Neigh!" Nina galloped fast into the house. "Neigh!"

"Oink!" Debbie trotted in behind her. Then they froze.

"I thought you said she wasn't going to be home," Nina said. "Can she hear?"

"Every word," Grandma Gert said.

"Meoowww, here comes the president!" Bonnie sprang into the house. Then she stopped.

"There's no meeting today," Libby said. She was afraid to look at anybody.

"Meoowwww, we've got to have the meeting!" Bonnie cried. She looked at Grandma Gert. "Can she hear me?"

Right then Grandma Gert couldn't hear a thing.

"You're cheating!" Bonnie whispered to Libby. "You knew your grandma was going to be home. You just lied so you could stall and I wouldn't be sworn in as president today!"

"Did not!" Libby said. "I know my grandma didn't kiss Boris. I don't even care if I'm president!"

"Aggh, Libby," Grandma Gert mumbled.

Just then Boris ran back into the kitchen. He licked up the mashed potatoes on the floor as fast as he could. Grandma Gert grabbed for her toilet plunger, but it was stuck in mashed potatoes.

"Boris, come now!" Annie commanded. "I mean it!"

Boris looked at Annie. Then he chased Grandma Gert around the table. His face was covered with mashed potatoes.

"*Libby!*" Grandma Gert hollered.

"Don't be afraid, Grandma!" Libby cried.

"Don't run!" Annie Bananie said. "Trust me, Grandma Gert. Just stand still!"

And then suddenly Grandma Gert stopped running. She leaned up against the counter. Boris stopped, too. But before anyone could stop Boris, he jumped up on

Grandma Gert. He licked her on the mouth. Then he ran back under the piano. Everybody froze. Grandma Gert had a white mustache, and her lips were covered with mashed potatoes. Grandma Gert held on to the counter and caught her breath.

"Oh my gosh, Grandma," Libby said. "I'm sorry. Are you okay?"

Right then Grandma Gert couldn't hear a thing.

"Oh my gosh, Libby." Annie Bananie giggled. "Your grandma just kissed Boris!"

"She did!" Nina galloped around the table. "I can't believe it! I'm going crazy!"

Grandma Gert looked at Nina. Then she licked the mashed potatoes off her lips.

"Oink," Debbie squealed. "Grandma Gert and Boris are girlfriend and boyfriend! Can she hear?"

Grandma Gert looked at Annie. Then she winked.

"Libby's still president!" Annie shouted. Her voice was big and happy.

"Hisss!" Bonnie shot her arm out at Annie Bananie like there was a claw at the end of it. "No way! This is just another trick!"

"Trick?" Grandma Gert said suddenly. "Me kiss a dog? Believe you me, that would have *had* to be a magic trick! I can't believe it." She giggled.

Libby just stood there. She was astonished.

"Oink." Debbie pushed her glasses up on her nose. "It's not too late. Libby should be sworn in as president."

"Grandma Gert, do you want to be vice president?" Annie Bananie asked.

"Are you kidding? Vice president?" Grandma Gert asked. "I'm president of my own club!" She untied her apron. "Aggh," she said. "I've got to hurry and get to my card game."

"Neigh," Nina said. "Let's swear Libby in!"

"Outside!" Grandma Gert said. "And take that dog with you!"

"*Meow,* okay, but I'm automatic vice president!" Bonnie shouted. "Come on, everybody. Follow me!"

Then everyone ran outside. Everybody but Annie Bananie and Libby.

"I'm president! Thank you, Grandma." Libby hugged Grandma Gert. "You're the best grandma in the whole world!"

"Just the world?" Grandma Gert laughed.

"Was it as bad kissing a dog as you thought it would be?" Annie asked. "Can you see how smart he is?"

"Aggh." Grandma Gert laughed.

"Since you kissed Boris, now do you think I could get a dog of my own?" Libby asked.

Grandma Gert started picking up mashed potatoes. Right then she couldn't hear a thing.

"Let's go, Madam President," Annie Bananie said.

Libby ran outside after Annie. She looked down at her necklace. It was sparkly. Like diamonds.

About the Author

Leah Komaiko is the author of many popular books for children, including *Earl's Too Cool for Me*, *I Like the Music*, and the bestselling *Annie Bananie*. *Annie Bananie Moves to Barry Avenue* is Leah Komaiko's first chapter book.

She lives in Los Angeles.